MARC BROWN

ARTHUR

Chapter Books 1-3

Read all the
Marc Brown Arthur Chapter Books!

Chapter Books 1-3

Arthur's Mystery Envelope

Arthur and the Scare-Your-Pants-Off Club

Arthur Makes the Team

Text by Stephen Krensky

Based on teleplays by Sheilarae Carpentier Lau, Terence Taylor, and Tom Hertz

Little, Brown and Company

Boston   New York   London

First Edition

The characters and events portrayed in this book are fictitious.
Any similarity to real persons, living or dead, is coincidental and not
intended by the author.

Arthur® is a registered trademark of Marc Brown.

Text has been reviewed by Laurel S. Ernst, M.A., Teachers College,
Columbia University, New York, New York; reading specialist,
Chappaqua, New York

Little, Brown originally published *Arthur's Mystery Envelope* (1998),
Arthur and the Scare-Your-Pants-Off Club (1998), and *Arthur Makes
the Team* (1998) as individual chapter books.

ISBN 0-316-12096-0

Library of Congress Control Number 00-105515

10 9 8 7 6 5 4 3 2 1

CW
WOR

Printed in the United States of America

For Maria Modugno

Contents

• • • • • • • • • •

Arthur's
Mystery Envelope

Chapter 1

• • • • • • • • • • •

The cafeteria at Lakewood Elementary was filled with kids eating lunch. Some of them had brought sandwiches from home. The rest were eating school lunches. Today's choices featured a mystery meat covered in gravy.

A few teachers wandered between the tables trying to keep the noise under control.

"Let's keep it down," said Mr. Ratburn. He shook his head. "I don't think anyone's listening."

Miss Sweetwater nodded. "Or maybe they just can't hear us," she said.

At one of the middle tables, Arthur and his friends were finishing up.

Arthur was poking at his food with a fork. "Even without the gravy," he said, "we'd have no idea where this came from."

"Ready for action, boys?" Francine asked.

"Ready," said Arthur. He put aside his tray.

"And waiting," said Buster.

They started a game of milk hockey. Francine and Sue Ellen made up one team. Arthur and Buster were the other. They used a crushed milk carton as a puck, hitting it back and forth the length of the table.

Francine dodged left and flipped the carton past Arthur's hand. Buster tried to stop it, but the puck slid past him off the table.

"Goal!" said Muffy. She was the official scorekeeper.

Francine smiled. "That didn't take long," she said.

Arthur flexed his hands. "We just take a little while to warm up."

"All right," said Sue Ellen. "Let us know when you're nice and toasty."

"Maybe we'll need a substitution," said Buster. He turned to Binky Barnes. "Do you want a turn?"

"No," said Binky, crushing another carton with his fist. He just liked making pucks.

"Attention, please!"

Miss Tingley, the school secretary, was speaking over the loudspeaker.

"Arthur Read, please report to Principal Haney's office immediately."

A hush fell over the room. Everyone was staring at Arthur. Buster's mouth was wide open. Binky's hand had frozen in mid-crush.

"Uh-oh!" said Francine.

"I'll say," said Muffy.

Sue Ellen just shook her head.

"You're in real trouble now, Arthur," said Buster. Sometimes Mr. Haney yelled at him for running through the halls. But he had been to the *office* only once — for putting sneezing powder on Mr. Ratburn's desk.

"Are you all right, Arthur?" Francine asked.

"I-I guess."

"He doesn't look all right," said Sue Ellen. "He looks like one of those deer you read about. The ones who stare into the car headlights."

"He's in shock," said Binky. "He's not used to visiting the principal's office. I could get there blindfolded with one hand tied behind my back."

"What did you do, Arthur?" asked Francine.

Arthur shook his head. "I don't know. Nothing that I can think of."

Binky snorted. "Don't bother trying that excuse on Mr. Haney. It never works for me."

Arthur stood up. "Well, I guess I should go."

"Nice knowing you, Arthur," said Francine.

"Good luck," said Buster. "And if you're not planning to finish those potatoes . . ." He pointed to Arthur's plate.

Arthur slid over his tray. "Help yourself," he said. "I just lost my appetite."

Chapter 2

• • • • • • • • • • • •

When Arthur got back to the classroom, his friends rushed to his side.

"You survived!" said Buster.

"With no obvious signs of torture," Binky added. He looked a little disappointed.

"What happened?" asked Francine.

Arthur let out a sigh. "Mr. Haney gave me this." He held up a large brown envelope. "He said it was for my mom."

"That's it?" asked Muffy. She reached out for a closer look. "What does it say? Is it sealed?"

Francine grabbed the envelope. "It's sealed, all right." She held it up to the light. "And too thick to read through."

"Give it a shake," said Buster, cocking his ears.

Francine shook the envelope for a moment. It rustled softly. "That doesn't tell us much," she said.

Binky folded his arms. "Let's just open it."

"I can't," said Arthur. "It's addressed to my mother. And look what's stamped on it: PRIVATE and CONFIDENTIAL."

"That's a bad sign," said Buster. "Good news is never private."

"Besides," said Binky, "you can't start making excuses until you know what kind of trouble you're in."

"Didn't Mr. Haney give you any clues at all?" Francine asked.

"He said it was important," said Arthur,

taking back the envelope. "That was about it."

"If it was good news," said Muffy, "Mr. Haney would have told you. My mother always tells me right away if we've gotten a new limousine or if the cook is making a special dessert for dinner."

"He didn't say anything like that," Arthur admitted.

"That means it's bad news," said Francine. "The question is, how bad is it?"

This was not a question Arthur wanted to think about.

Binky laughed. "Oooooh! I'll bet you lost a library book."

"I don't think Mr. Haney gets involved with overdue library books," said Arthur. "Besides, I just returned all mine."

"Oh, no!" said Francine.

"What?" said Muffy.

"Tell us," said Buster.

"Tell me!" said Arthur.

"Never mind," said Francine. "It's too terrible to think about."

Arthur turned pale. "That's why you have to tell me."

"All right," said Francine. "But you forced me into it." She shuddered. "What if you didn't pass Mr. Ratburn's history test?"

Arthur frowned. The big test had been the week before. It had been a hard one.

"Remember, Arthur? You told me afterward that you wrote how the Pilgrims came to America in 1620."

"Francine, the Pilgrims *did* come to America in 1620."

She looked surprised. "Really?"

Everyone else nodded.

"Well, still . . ." Francine tapped the envelope. "The proof is right here. And if you failed that test, you might fail the whole year. You know what that means: summer school."

Arthur sat down in his chair and thought about his fate. Summer school. Perhaps the two most dreaded words in the English language.

He saw himself chained to the wall of a dark dungeon. Outside the barred window, he could hear his friends playing. He looked out through the bars. Buster and the Brain were setting up a tent for camping. Muffy and Prunella were Rollerblading.

Arthur looked around his cell. He was alone — with only some thick, dusty books for company. Then the guard, Mr. Ratburn, walked in. He was slurping ice cream from a cone. A few drops fell on the stones, just beyond Arthur's reach.

"Snap out of it, Arthur!" said Buster.

Arthur looked at his friend blankly.

"You know what they say," Buster went

on. "Those who don't learn their history are doomed to repeat it."

Arthur sighed. History or not, he felt doomed for sure.

Chapter 3

• • • • • • • • • • •

Arthur could have taken the envelope straight home after school. But he didn't.

"Mr. Haney didn't say anything about *when* you should deliver the envelope," the Brain had told him. "Under international law, you have the right to make a plan."

They were sitting in a booth at the Sugar Bowl. Buster and Francine were there, too. Prunella and Muffy were seated behind them.

Arthur had bought some candy, but he wasn't eating it. He was just moving it around in front of him. The candy was shaped in a rectangle with a big question mark inside it.

The Brain was staring hard at Arthur's envelope. "If only I could use X-ray vision . . . ," he said.

Buster grabbed the envelope from him. "We have to take action! I don't want to spend all summer doing fun stuff without you." He pushed the envelope toward the edge of the table. "Hey, what if you accidentally lost it?"

He shoved the envelope onto the floor.

"It could end up in the trash. Or a shredder. Then bulldozed into a landfill. Only the seagulls would read it there. And we don't have to worry what they think."

"That's true," said Arthur.

Prunella picked up the envelope.

"Don't listen to him, Arthur. He doesn't look ahead. You need to think of something that won't be blamed on you in the end." She paused. "Maybe you could hide

17

it in the laundry basket — and it could get *washed*." She picked up the envelope and held it carefully as if it were wet and dripping. "She won't be able to read it, but you won't be blamed."

"Laundry," said Arthur. "Interesting."

"Not interesting," said Muffy. "Risky. You need to get it as far away from your house as possible. Buy it a first-class ticket to Alaska or Timbuktu."

"I don't have that kind of money," said Arthur.

He looked at the clock. It was time to go home.

Everyone went outside.

Francine was still frowning. "There must be some way out of this," she said.

The Brain looked down at the storm drain. "You could drop it in here," he said. "The current would carry it into Bear Lake and from there to the Otter River. Once it

was in the harbor, it would be carried out to sea — maybe even to Europe. When it eventually washed up on shore, it's possible a mother might find it. But she probably wouldn't understand English, so you'd be safe."

"Europe is far away," said Arthur.

Francine plucked the envelope from the Brain's hand. "Don't do it, Arthur," she said. "If you try to lose it, you'll be in double trouble — for losing it *and* for whatever you did in the first place."

She handed the envelope back to him.

"The whole thing doesn't seem fair," said Arthur. "I didn't do anything! I'll just have to give the envelope to my mother and see what happens."

He had hoped saying that would make him feel better. It didn't.

"That's a last resort," said the Brain. "But, of course, the choice is yours."

Chapter 4

• • • • • • • • • • • • •

"Hello!" Arthur called out softly.

No one was in the kitchen except his dog, Pal. Arthur knew his mother was home, though. Her car was in the driveway.

"But she could be busy," he told Pal. "In fact, I'm sure of it. She could be working or helping D.W. or taking care of baby Kate. I don't want to disturb her."

Pal barked.

"Are you hungry?" said Arthur.

Pal wagged his tail.

Arthur put down his backpack on the counter. One corner of Mr. Haney's envelope was sticking out of the flap. Then he began rinsing out Pal's food dish.

"Mr. Haney told me the envelope was for Mom," Arthur explained to Pal. "But he didn't say what was in it."

Pal barked.

"No," said Arthur, "I can't eat the envelope."

Pal barked again.

"No, I can't bury it in the backyard, either."

He put the empty dish on the floor. Pal whined with disappointment.

"All my friends think the news must be bad," Arthur went on.

Pal continued to whine.

"Francine thinks I failed Mr. Ratburn's history test. She says I'll have to go to summer school." Arthur made a face.

Pal jumped up and down at his side.

Arthur fetched the dog food from the pantry. "Maybe I'll just leave it out and not say anything. Mr. Haney said I should bring it home to her. He didn't say I actually had to *give* it to her. Maybe she won't even notice it."

Arthur lay the dish on the table, then opened his backpack. He removed the envelope carefully and put it on the table.

"What's that?"

Arthur whirled around to find his sister D.W. standing in the doorway.

"What's what?"

D.W. pointed. "The envelope, silly."

"Nothing!" he shouted. He leaned on the table. "It's just a dumb old envelope. People could walk by this envelope for weeks and not even notice it. And even if they did notice it, they wouldn't bother to open a boring envelope like this."

"That's a lot of nothing," said D.W. "You sure are acting weird."

"I'm not acting weird," said Arthur. He straightened up and folded his arms. "I'm worried. I mean, I'm not worried. I'm hurried. That's it. Hurried. Third grade is very busy."

D.W. climbed onto a chair and stared into Arthur's eyes. "You don't fool me," she said. "I know *worry* when I see it."

Arthur blinked. "You do?"

D.W. nodded. "Yup. You get wrinkles."

"I do?"

She nodded. "I'm not surprised. You could worry about lots of things. Like maybe someday you'll be too old for birthday presents. Or maybe you think there really is a boogeyman, and he's just waiting for the first night you forget to check under your bed."

Arthur sighed. "Those are regular worries. Everyday worries. I can handle those."

D.W. gave him a careful look. "You mean there's *more?* Come on, spill the beans."

"All right, all right!" said Arthur. "The principal just gave me this envelope for Mom. That's all. Now leave me alone!"

But D.W. wasn't finished yet. She took a look at the envelope. "What are these words?" she asked.

"Which words?"

"These big words on the front."

"PRIVATE and CONFIDENTIAL."

D.W. frowned. "I know PRIVATE. What does CON-FI-DEN-TEE-UL mean?"

Arthur sighed. "That only Mom can look at it."

D.W.'s eyes opened wide. She got down from the chair and skipped toward the hall, singing,

> *"Arthur's in trouble,*
> *Arthur's in trouble."*

For once Arthur didn't argue with her. He knew she was right.

Chapter 5

•••••••••••

The good news was that D.W. suddenly stopped singing. The bad news was that she stopped because she had bumped into her mother.

"Slow down, sweetie. We can't afford to put a traffic light in here."

Mrs. Read gave D.W. a quick kiss. Her hands were full of papers.

"What a day! If I had two heads and four hands, I'd still be behind."

Mrs. Read was an accountant. She always got a little frazzled at tax time.

"Mom, Arthur's acting a little weird. He brought home a —"

"Hey!" said Arthur. "That's none of your —"

"Hush, Arthur!" said his mother. "Not now, D.W. I've got a few calls to make."

She put her papers down on the counter.

"Arthur, what is this?"

Arthur cringed. "That?"

"Yes, that." She pointed to the envelope and Pal's dish beside it. "On the table."

"The table? Here? In the kitchen?"

His mother folded her arms. "Yes, the kitchen table. Since when does Pal eat there?"

Arthur let out a deep breath.

"He doesn't."

"Then why did you leave his dish on the table?" She put it down on the floor. "Honestly, Arthur, I expect you to be more careful."

While Arthur fidgeted, Mrs. Read picked up the phone and dialed a number. She left a message with the secretary.

"That's my third try this afternoon. That man is just impossible to reach." She glanced at Arthur. "Is everything all right? You look a little pale."

"Of course," said Arthur. "I was just thinking about, um . . . setting the table for dinner." He pulled out some forks and knives from a drawer and began placing them in front of each chair.

"Mail call!" said Mr. Read, arriving with a bundle of letters. He dropped them on top of Arthur's envelope.

"How is everyone today?"

"Dear, you have whipped cream behind your ear."

"Really? I thought I had cleaned it all up." He scraped the cream off with his finger. "I was experimenting with a new dessert."

Mr. Read was very busy with his catering business.

"I hope no one was hurt," said Mrs. Read.

Mr. Read sighed. "Only the piecrust didn't survive."

The phone rang.

"I'll get it," said Mrs. Read. She picked up the mail and the envelope as she answered the phone. "Hello? Oh, hi, Leah."

She started to look through the mail.

One letter went into the wastebasket.

"No, no, I'm not disappointed you called. I was just expecting to hear from Herb."

She put a bill aside for later.

"I needed some paperwork from him."

She flipped through a magazine.

"Yes, I know. It's all due Monday."

Arthur watched his mother with an increasing sense of doom. He edged his way to the door. His mother had reached Mr. Haney's envelope.

Suddenly the water on the stove began bubbling over.

"Oh, I've got to run," said Mrs. Read. "Talk to you later, Leah." She hung up the phone and dropped the envelope on the edge of the counter. She turned back to the stove.

The envelope teetered for a moment — and then fell into the wastebasket.

Arthur slumped with relief. He was innocent. He hadn't put the envelope in the trash. Some other hand had guided it there. It was fate. It was destiny. It was meant to be.

Chapter 6

● ● ● ● ● ● ● ● ● ● ●

Dinner was hard to swallow. How could Arthur concentrate on eating? Every time he looked up, he saw the envelope peeking at him from the wastebasket.

Even the fact that they were having hamburgers and potato puffs hadn't cheered him up. His partly eaten hamburger sat on the edge of his plate like a crescent moon. Usually he piled the potato puffs into a castle wall and then lined up the green beans like alligators in the moat. But tonight he had only stamped the puffs and beans down with his fork. They looked like little shredded carpets.

"Are you trying to save wear and tear on your teeth, Arthur?" asked his mother.

Arthur looked confused.

She pointed to his plate. "All that mashing. You still have to eat them, you know. We don't want to waste food."

Arthur took a small bite.

His father helped himself to some salad. "You're awfully quiet tonight, Arthur," he said.

Arthur squirmed in his chair. "We worked hard in school today." He looked at his father. "When you were in school, were tests important?"

"Oh, yes. We didn't have all the different projects you kids have today. Sometimes a single test could be half our whole grade."

"That much?"

His father smiled. "Definitely. I wouldn't

say you kids have it easy, but you do have more choices."

"Most important," said Mrs. Read, "we want you to do your best."

"I always do my best," said D.W., who was swapping potato puffs with Kate. "It's all part of my plan."

"What plan is that, sweetie?" asked her mother.

"Her plan for world domination," said Arthur.

"Arrrthur!" said his father.

"Sorry." Arthur changed the subject. "Do you think every part of school is important? I mean, don't some parts matter more than others?"

Mr. Read shook his head. "That's hard to say. At your age I never planned on having a catering business. And even though my business is food, I still need to know math for planning and how to write for advertising."

"What about, um, history?" said Arthur. "That wouldn't matter so much, would it?"

"History's important, too," said his father. "I might want to study old recipes or create a meal with some historical theme."

"I see," said Arthur, wishing he didn't.

"It makes sense to learn about everything," said his mother. "You can't tell when it might come in handy later on." She looked down the table. "Arthur, pass me the potato puffs, please."

Arthur picked up the bowl.

D.W. smiled. "Arthur, isn't there anything else you'd like to give Mom while you're at it?"

Arthur just barely kept himself from kicking D.W. under the table. "Just my thanks," he said, "for making this great dinner."

He forked up some mashed puffs and beans and filled his mouth.

His mother looked at him. "Thank you, Arthur — I think."

She might have said more, but the phone rang. She jumped up to get it.

Saved by the bell, thought Arthur — at least for now.

Chapter 7

• • • • • • • • • • •

After dinner, Arthur went to his room to do his homework.

Think of a word that rhymes with rope *and* hope.

"Arrghhh!" said Arthur.

He switched quickly to math. The first problem involved cutting a rectangle in half.

"I wish I could cut that envelope in half," said Arthur.

Another question was about a mailbag filled with letters. There was no mention of the *E* word, but that was all Arthur could think about.

He began doodling on the edge of his paper. He started with a big rectangle, an enormous rectangle, the largest rectangle in the world.

But was it only a rectangle? No, it was a giant envelope, and it was chasing Arthur down a hill. It tumbled end over end. Arthur could barely keep ahead of it.

"Don't run," the envelope was saying. "I know you'll fit nicely inside me. And don't worry. I will never let you out."

"No, thank you," said Arthur. "I'll get flattened." He ran faster.

"That's not my fault," said the envelope, huffing and puffing. "I'm just not in very good shape."

Arthur rubbed his eyes. He needed a break.

He took a peek in Kate's room. She was already asleep.

"Babies are lucky," he muttered. "They

don't have to worry about envelopes. Or history tests. Or summer school. They only have to look cute and fill their diapers."

Kate turned in her sleep, and her blanket slipped off her.

Arthur put it back. "The good old days," he sighed.

His mother was sitting in her office. She was chewing on a pencil and humming while she worked. Arthur tiptoed past the door. He found his father and D.W. watching *The Karaoke Kittens* show on TV.

The kittens were wearing straw hats and dancing in a line while they sang.

"Those kittens are crazy," said D.W. "Watch carefully now. This is the best part."

"How do you know?" asked her father.

Arthur sat down. "She's seen this episode eighty-four times," he explained.

"And it just gets better and better," said D.W. She shook her head in time with the music.

Her father hummed along. "Not every kitten can dance like that," he pointed out. "It takes a lot of practice."

A commercial came on.

"Is the stress of everyday life getting you down?"

Arthur nodded.

"Do you feel like you're no longer in control?"

Arthur nodded again.

"The pounding, the pounding. It just won't stop."

Arthur cradled his head in his arms.

"For the chance to feel like your old self again, try Painfree or Painfree Plus. Headache relief is just minutes away."

Arthur stood up. If only he could take a pill to get rid of his problem. But things were not that easy.

"You really look tired, Arthur," said his father.

"I am," Arthur admitted.

"Sshhhh!" said D.W. "The kittens are going to sing 'Fur Ball.' I love that song."

Arthur didn't stay to hear it. With a quiet "Good night," he went up to bed.

Chapter 8

• • • • • • • • • • • •

As Arthur got ready for bed, he found himself looking at his pillow. He had never noticed before how much it looked like a stuffed envelope.

While brushing his teeth, Arthur brought his face right up to the mirror. His teeth lined up in little square rows.

Almost like envelopes, he thought.

Everywhere he looked — the wallpaper, the carpeting, the pattern on his blanket — he saw envelopes. They came in every shape and size.

"I have envelopes on the brain," he

decided. "What I need is a good night's sleep."

Arthur climbed into bed and pulled up the covers.

"Are you still awake, Arthur?"

D.W. was standing in the doorway.

"No. I'm sound asleep. You're a bad dream. Go away."

"If you're sound asleep, how can you tell me to go away?"

Arthur sat up. "What do you want?"

"I want to know about the trouble you're in."

"There's no trouble, D.W."

She was not convinced. "What was in that mysterious envelope?"

"I don't know," Arthur said honestly.

"Mom didn't mention it to you?"

"No, she didn't."

"Oh." D.W. was disappointed. "Don't worry. I'm sure you'll get in trouble for something else."

"Thanks, D.W. That makes me feel much better."

"Anytime," said D.W., and went back to her room.

Arthur stared at the ceiling. Strictly speaking, he had told D.W. the truth. His mother *hadn't* mentioned to him what was inside the envelope. Of course, that was only because she hadn't *seen* it yet. The envelope was still sitting in the wastebasket.

Why can't it just stay there? thought Arthur.

He closed his eyes for what seemed like only a second.

His eyes opened.

Arthur heard some paper rustling. What was making that sound? He got out of bed and listened.

The sound was coming from downstairs.

Arthur followed the noise into the kitchen. The wastebasket was shaking — as if something was bouncing around inside it. Arthur looked down. Mr. Haney's envelope was growing bigger right before his eyes! The wastebasket could no longer hold it.

Arthur pulled the envelope free and ran upstairs. The envelope was flapping in his arms. It was getting too big to carry. Arthur dragged it along the floor to the bathroom. He hoisted it into the tub and drew the shower curtain.

The curtain shook and trembled.

Arthur screamed — and fled downstairs into his mother's arms.

"What's going on?" she asked.

Arthur grabbed her arm and pulled.

"We have to get out of the house, Mom. It's getting too big!"

As they stepped outside, one corner of the envelope wriggled through a window. Another popped out of the chimney.

"What's going on?" asked his mother.

"It's the envelope," yelled Arthur. "Don't open it! It could be something horrible!"

At that moment the roof flew off the house. The top of the envelope rose up, and the flap opened.

D.W. popped out.

"You tricked me, Arthur," she said. "You haven't even told Mom yet."

"Noooooo!" cried Arthur.

Chapter 9

•••••••••••

Arthur woke up. His hands were crossed in front of his face.

"I can't go on this way," he muttered. "Even summer school would be better than this."

He walked downstairs. His father was still watching TV. It was some kind of cooking show.

"Parsley, sage, rosemary, and thyme may make for a good song title, but don't use them together as seasonings."

"It might be worth trying," Mr. Read said to himself. "Maybe in a soup . . ."

Arthur kept going. His feet felt like lead,

and his legs seemed to be moving in slow motion.

The envelope was still in the wastebasket. Arthur picked it out.

He walked over to the dining room, where his mother had her work area.

The light was still on.

Arthur took a deep breath. "It's going to keep bothering me until I get this over with."

He entered the dining room.

"Do you have a second, Mom?"

His mother put down her pen. "For you, two seconds. But why are you up so late?"

Arthur took a deep breath. "That's what I need to talk to you about. I was supposed to do something right away when I got home. But I was worried I might be in trouble, so I didn't do it, and now I'm afraid you're going to get mad —"

"Slow down, Arthur! What's going on? You can tell me. I won't get mad."

"Promise?"

She nodded.

Arthur handed her the envelope. She slit it open and glanced inside.

"Ah! Here it is!" She frowned. "Arthur, I've been waiting for this all night."

Arthur looked down at the floor. "You said you wouldn't get mad."

"Yes, yes, I did." His mother took a deep breath. "Well, I'm not mad exactly. *Frustrated* would be a better word. I'm very frustrated. I've been trying to reach Herb for hours. I need this information."

"But this is from Mr. Haney."

"Herb is his first name."

She glanced through the papers.

"Um, Mom?"

"Hmmmm. . . . Yes, Arthur?"

"What's in there?"

His mother looked up. "Tax documents. I'm doing his tax return."

"Nothing to do with me?"

"Not unless you want to help Mr. Haney pay his taxes!"

Arthur laughed. "Good-bye, summer school," he murmured.

Mrs. Read put down her papers for a moment. "Now I think I understand," she said. "But Arthur, even if this was about you, we would need to know."

"What if it was something bad?"

His mother sighed. "Putting off bad news doesn't make it get any better. And sometimes it makes it worse. Besides, Dad and I can't help you with a problem if we don't know you have one."

Arthur nodded. "I guess that's true."

"Well, we can talk more in the morning. Now back to bed, honey. It's late."

She gave him a kiss.

All that worrying for nothing, thought Arthur. He had tortured himself all afternoon and evening for no good reason.

"Cheer up, Arthur," said his mother.

"You're not disappointed, I hope. Because if you really want to be in trouble, I'm sure I could arrange —"

"Good night, Mom!" Arthur said hurriedly, and bolted for the door.

Chapter 10

• • • • • • • • • • • • •

It was too late for Arthur to call his friends, but he could imagine their reactions.

"You're still alive?" Francine would say. "Way to go!"

Buster would be pleased, too. "Now we'll be together all summer! If you get in any trouble then, I'll be right there beside you."

"Rats," Binky would say. "You got off the hook again? I can't believe it."

As Arthur was about to head up the stairs, he saw D.W. waiting for him.

"So, tell me what happened!" she said.

"Are you grounded for a year? Off to jail? Can I have your room?"

"Back to bed, you two!" their mother called out.

"I'm just getting a drink," said D.W. She stared at Arthur. "I'm waiting. . . ."

Arthur shrugged. "Sorry to disappoint you, D.W., but there's nothing to tell. I don't know where you get these crazy ideas."

"Crazy ideas? Where do I get them?" She stopped to think. "Let me see. I wasn't the one frozen in terror. Or jumpy as a frog."

"Frozen? Jumpy?" Arthur's eyes opened wide. "What an imagination!"

"Come on," said D.W. "Tell me. Are you moving into the garage? Is Pal moving there with you? Are we —"

"Enough questions," said Arthur. "I'm not telling you anything."

"You're not?"

Arthur smiled. "D.W., this is one mystery you'll have to solve on your own."

She made a face at him, but Arthur didn't care. He felt better at last.

Arthur and the Scare-Your-Pants-Off Club

Chapter 1

• • • • • • • • • • •

"I'm hungry," said D.W.

She was sitting in the kitchen, waiting for breakfast.

"Be patient, sweetie," said her mother. "Your father's almost ready."

D.W. drummed her fingers on the table. She didn't like to be patient. It took too long. And the only thing worse than being patient was being *told* to be patient.

"Just another moment," said Mr. Read. He was busy at the stove. "Lightly browned . . . a little powdered sugar . . ."

"Yummm," said D.W. She licked her lips.

"Yummm, yummm," said baby Kate in her high chair. She licked her lips, too.

"Don't take too long, dear," said Mrs. Read. "The kids are revving up."

Mr. Read picked up the platter and brought it toward the table. "Ta-dah!" he announced. "By special request, my World-Famous Whoopee Waffles. The favorite of presidents, professional athletes, and rock stars. There's whole-grain goodness in every bite."

"Whoopee!" said D.W.

"Now, if I could just have your plates, I'll be happy to serve —"

Arthur rushed in.

"Morning, Mom, Dad . . . Gotta run. Oops!"

Arthur unexpectedly collided with his father, knocking the waffles high into the air.

D.W. gasped.

Arthur pointed.

But Mr. Read sprang into action. He caught the falling waffles on the platter, then dished them onto the table.

D.W. clapped. "My hero!" she said.

Her father took a bow. "Lucky I spent that summer waiting on tables in the Catskills."

"More," said baby Kate.

Mr. Read smiled. "I don't think so, honey. Let's not push my luck."

"Sorry," said Arthur. "I guess I wasn't looking where I was going."

"I guess not," his mother agreed. "But why are you in such a hurry?"

Arthur sat down to eat. "I have to get to the library." He stuffed half of a waffle into his mouth.

"Slow down a little," said his mother. "Drink some juice. You don't want to choke. What's at the library that can't wait for waffles?"

"The new Scare-Your-Pants-Off Club

book will be there today. I want to be first in line."

Mrs. Read was impressed. "You're going to the library? On a Saturday? Of your own free will?"

"Wow!" said his father. "Hard to argue with that. But aren't you exaggerating a little? Are these books really flying off the shelves?"

"Just about," said Arthur. "They're really popular. I waited three weeks for the last one."

"Why do you think everyone likes them so much?" asked his mother.

Arthur wasn't sure. "Maybe it's because they're sort of scary and fun at the same time."

"An unusual combination," said Mr. Read.

"Right," said Arthur. He swallowed another bite and dashed for the door.

Then he was gone.

"I don't see what the big deal is," said D.W. "But I think it's great that Arthur is going to the library."

"Why is that?" asked her mother.

D.W. eyed the platter. "Because," she said, "it leaves more waffles for me!"

Chapter 2

• • • • • • • • • • • •

Arthur hurried down the street. He was thinking about the new book he would soon be reading. He wondered how he would get the pants scared off him this time. Last month's *Which Witch Is Which?* had started him shivering by the third page.

Arthur jumped high over a storm grate. He didn't want some creature from the Underworld rising through the holes to grab him. It was just that sort of carelessness that had cost Susie so dearly in *Night of the Cornstalker*.

Arthur turned the corner and saw the library ahead of him.

"Oh, no!"

Outside the building, a long line of kids had already formed. It snaked down the stairs and along the sidewalk.

"Hi, Arthur!"

"Over here!"

At the end of the line, Francine, Buster, Sue Ellen, and the Brain were waving to him.

Arthur trudged over to join them. The line was so long! It was unbelievable.

"Guess we should have met earlier," said Francine.

"Yeah," said the Brain. "Like just before dawn."

"Hey!" said Buster. "Let's not jump to conclusions. Who knows? Maybe they're just all here to study."

"On a Saturday?" said Francine.

Sue Ellen yawned. "*Early* on a Saturday?" she added.

Arthur sighed. "I don't think so, Buster. Besides, everyone I just passed is wearing a SYPOC shirt or hat."

"Even once we get in," said Francine, "there won't be any new books left."

"I guess we could check out some of the old ones to read again," said Arthur.

Buster nodded. "Yeah. How about *Curse of the Mummy's Breath?* Talk about not brushing your teeth . . ."

"Or *Skeletons in the Closet,*" said the Brain. "I wore the same clothes for a week after I read that one."

The clouds rolled overhead, and the sun disappeared.

"Don't forget the scariest one of all," said Francine. "*Zombie Substitute Teacher.*"

"Oooooh!" everyone said together.

They all shuddered.

"I wonder why that TV truck is here," said Buster. He pointed across the street.

"Maybe the reporters are fans, too," said Sue Ellen.

"Or maybe," said the Brain, "it's news to see a line outside a library on a Saturday morning."

"Never mind that," said Francine. "Look! The doors are opening."

They all turned to watch. The library doors creaked open slowly. A sinister shadow appeared within, slowly moving forward. The sun came back out as the shadow reached the steps.

"Good morning," said Ms. Turner, the librarian. "This is quite a turnout."

The kids cheered.

She held up a hand to quiet the crowd.

"It's a pleasure to see you all. However, I have some bad news. Anyone who has come to check out the new Scare-Your-Pants-Off Club book today will be unable

to do so. In fact, all of the books in that series have been removed from our shelves until further notice."

The kids were stunned. They let out a shriek of disbelief.

"I've been waiting for an hour!"

"No fair!"

"What happened?"

Ms. Turner held a finger to her lips. "That's all I can say at this time. Naturally you're all welcome to come in and pick out something else. But quietly. Remember, this is a library."

She went back inside.

The doors closed behind her — and nobody rushed to open them again.

Chapter 3

• • • • • • • • • • •

"I don't get it," said Arthur as the kids walked away. "Who would want to get rid of our books?"

"Not all our books," Francine reminded him. "Just the Scare-Your-Pants-Off Club books."

"Why pick on them?" asked Buster.

Nobody had a quick answer.

"Hey!" said Sue Ellen. "Look at that!"

She pointed to a TV store across the street. The SYPOC logo filled the screen.

Everyone crossed the street to find out what was going on.

"*In suburban Elwood City,*" said the

news reporter, *"a parents group has chased some children's books off the shelves of the public library."*

The picture showed the library and all the kids waiting in line.

"That's us," said the Brain.

"How did we get on TV so fast?" asked Buster.

"I imagine," said the Brain, "that they used a satellite downfeed to get these pictures back to the studio."

"Shhh!" said Francine. "I want to hear the rest."

"The parents group, called PAWS — Parents Against Weird Stories — says the scary stories are bad for kids. We tried unsuccessfully to reach E. A. D'Poe, the author of the books, for comment. Hoping to build more support, PAWS is holding a rally for concerned parents. They will meet on the library steps at one o'clock tomorrow afternoon."

The news moved on to other stories.

"Red alert!" Buster shouted. "If we ever want the pants scared off us again, we've got to do something — and fast."

"But what?" asked Francine.

The Brain scratched his head. "Generally speaking," he said, "minors have limited access to legal recourse or arbitration."

"Which means," said Arthur, "that there isn't much we can do." He looked around at his friends. "But I'm not willing to give up yet. We've never given up before!"

"Sure we have," said Buster.

"Lots of times," said Francine.

"We're good at giving up," said Sue Ellen.

"Not when it's important," said Arthur. "Remember the time you helped clean out my garage so I could go with you to see *Galaxy Avengers?*"

Arthur remembered it well.

Francine was carrying two heavy bags of trash. The Brain was stacking paint cans, and Arthur was lining up two-by-fours against the wall.

Buster was sweeping the floor. When he finished, he started balancing the broom on his nose. Suddenly the broom fell off, knocking over the two-by-fours. They fell onto the paint cans, which opened and spilled paint everywhere.

Francine was so startled that she dropped the trash bags, and all the garbage tumbled out.

"I remember that," said Francine. "Nice going, Buster!"

"It was an accident!" said Buster. "It could have happened to anyone."

"The point is," said Arthur, "we made it to the movie."

"The *next* day," said the Brain. "After we cleaned up everything."

"Okay," said Arthur, "so we hit a few

bumps along the way. What about the time Buster needed help with his math?"

Buster was sitting on his couch, deep in concentration. His homework and math books were spread out around him. "Come on, Buster," *said Arthur.* "You can get this."

He and Francine were wearing the numbers 7 and 3 on their chests. Pal was standing between them with an x, *the multiplication symbol, draped over him. The Brain had an equals sign taped to his forehead.*

"Think quickly," said the Brain. "My forehead is beginning to itch."

"Twenty-one!" said Buster. "The answer was twenty-one. I still remember it."

"See?" said Arthur.

"I'd forgotten about teaching Buster to multiply," said Francine. "If we can do that, maybe we can do this, too."

"I know," said Buster. "Let's go on strike! No more homework till we get our books back."

Arthur sighed.

The Brain folded his arms.

Francine rolled her eyes.

"All right, all right," said Buster. "It was worth a try. But who has a better idea?"

Nobody did — not yet, anyway.

Chapter 4

• • • • • • • • • • • •

Just after lunch Arthur, Buster, Francine, the Brain, and Sue Ellen met at the Sugar Bowl.

"What we need to do," said the Brain, "is quantitatively demonstrate that we're not alone in our opinion."

"Huh?" said Buster.

"He means," said Francine, "we have to show PAWS that a lot of kids want their books back."

"I wonder where Muffy is," said Francine. "I called and left a message for her to join us."

"We can't wait for her," said Buster.

"We have to move, move, move! We have to take action!"

"I have one idea," said Francine. "We could get signatures on a petition. That's what my mom did to save the old City Hall building. If we can show the PAWS people how much support the books have, maybe we can change their minds."

"But it can't just be kids' support," said the Brain. "We'll need adults, too."

"Do we have enough time?" said Sue Ellen. "The PAWS rally is tomorrow."

"Well," said Arthur, "there's only one way to find out."

The kids split into several groups and spread out through town. Buster and Arthur teamed up on Arthur's front lawn.

"Gooooood morning, Elwood City!" Buster shouted into a megaphone.

Two cars whizzed by without stopping.

"Step right up!" Buster went on. "See the Amazing Arthur perform feats of wonder! Then sign your name to save our books."

Arthur was wearing a diving mask and bathing suit. He was trying to balance on a rope above an inflatable wading pool.

"Buster, are you sure about this?" Arthur asked. He didn't feel very amazing. He didn't think he looked amazing, either.

"It's like a commercial," Buster whispered. "Before we can get them to sign, we have to get their attention. Now, go ahead!"

Arthur took a breath and started along the rope, balancing himself with a broom.

A few kids passing by stopped to watch.

"Easy, there!"

"Whoa! Back! Back!"

Arthur leaned one way, then the other. As the broom twirled like a propeller, he fell into the water.

The kids laughed. "Again! Again!" they shouted.

"The Amazing Arthur will be happy to perform again," said Buster. "But first a word from our sponsor."

He pulled out the petition and explained what they were trying to do.

While Arthur dried off with a towel, the kids signed their names.

Meanwhile, Francine and Sue Ellen were jumping double Dutch in the park. A line of kids was waiting for a turn to jump.

Francine was chanting,

"PAWS has taken our books away,
So I'm asking for your help today.
Line up now and sign your name.
That's the point of my rope game."

As each kid finished, he or she signed the petition.

"Next!" said Francine.

Over at the bus stop, the Brain was trying to educate the waiting passengers. He had covered a blackboard with flow charts, equations, and names of books.

"As you can see," he told the crowd, "we predict that the impact on school performance will be geometric. Note the marked rise in the learning curve."

He pointed with his pointer.

The bus passengers shook their heads. A few covered their ears.

"It is our hypothesis," the Brain went on, "that recreational reading yields many educational benefits. Therefore, we invite you to sign our petition."

"We'll sign," said someone, "if you promise to stop explaining things to us."

"Yes, please!"

"By all means."

"We agree."

They crowded around the Brain's clipboard.

He smiled. If everyone else was having the same success he was, they might have a chance after all.

Chapter 5

• • • • • • • • • • •

After Arthur and Buster had collected all
the signatures they could in the neighborhood, they went to the park to gather
more.

"Are you sure you don't want to be the
Amazing Arthur here, too?" Buster asked.

Arthur was sure. He had been amazing
enough for one day.

"Let's split up," he said. "That way we
can cover more ground."

Buster headed for the seating area
around the pond while Arthur set out
across the fields.

At first Arthur had trouble catching up

with people who were Rollerblading or biking or just playing games.

"Sorry, we're busy."

"Catch me later."

"Not now. We're at match point."

It was a little discouraging. He did spot an old woman tending some plants near a fountain. Finally, someone who wasn't on the move.

He walked over to introduce himself.

"Excuse me, ma'am," he said. "Could I speak to you for a moment?"

"You already are," said the woman. Her glasses were perched low on her nose. "It's a little late to ask my permission."

Arthur hesitated. "I guess that's true. It's for a good cause, though. At least we think it is."

"And what is this good cause, may I ask?"

"A parents group has had our favorite

books removed from the library," Arthur explained. "We're trying to get them back. But we want to show that a lot of people feel the same way we do. So we've started up this petition. Would you sign it for us?"

The woman paused. "I see I'm not the only one doing volunteer work today." She gave Arthur a long look. "It all depends on the books. I wouldn't want to go against your parents' wishes."

"Oh, you wouldn't be. My parents like me to read different things. My father says it's like the food groups. It's healthy to have a little bit of everything."

"Good advice," said the woman.

"Besides," said Arthur, "these books are our favorites: the Scare-Your-Pants-Off Club books."

The old woman sat back on her heels and pushed her glasses back up on her nose.

"Really? The Scare-Your-Pants-Off Club books? Do you read them . . . um . . . ?"

"Arthur." He shook her hand. "Do I read them? Of course! I haven't missed a single one."

The woman frowned. "Then the situation *is* serious. Maybe I should speak to this parents group myself!"

She stood up and gathered her gardening tools.

"Don't give up, Arthur. You and your friends are doing a good thing."

Arthur looked puzzled. "Sure. Thanks — I think . . ."

He watched her leave. Then he looked down at his clipboard. "Hey! Wait! You forgot to sign."

But the woman was gone.

Chapter 6

• • • • • • • • • • • •

Later that afternoon, Arthur, Francine, Sue Ellen, and Buster walked out of the Sugar Bowl, eating ice cream cones.

"Collecting signatures is hard work," said Buster.

"Do you think we have enough names?" asked Francine.

Arthur licked the drips around his cone. "I think so. There are pages and pages. I just hope PAWS will listen to us."

Francine looked at her watch. "I wonder where the Brain is. He was supposed to meet us at five."

"Look!" said Buster. "Here comes Muffy."

"Where has she been, anyway?" said Francine. "We could have used her help today."

Muffy was wearing a big smile. "Great news, everyone!" she announced. "My parents are having a big party tomorrow at WonderWorld." She paused. "And I can invite anyone I want."

"Wow!" said Arthur. WonderWorld was the best carnival and theme park around. Going there for free would be a real treat.

"That's terrific," said Sue Ellen.

"Count me in!" said Francine.

Francine noticed Muffy eyeing her cone.

"Want a lick?" she asked. She held out the cone.

Muffy backed away. "Um, no thanks. My mom won't let me — too much fat and sugar." She shut her eyes. "Take it away. Please!"

At that moment the Brain came around the corner. He was clutching a newspaper in one hand.

"Sorry I'm late, everyone. Wait till you hear what I just—" He stopped suddenly. "Oh . . . hello, Muffy."

Muffy looked at the sidewalk.

"What did you find out?" Francine asked.

The Brain glanced in Muffy's direction. "Listen to this," he said. "There's a whole article in today's paper about the book ban and an interview with the people behind it. I'll skip to the important part."

He started reading from the newspaper.

" 'Kids don't know the harm these books do,' said Millicent Crosswire. 'My poor daughter, Muffy, read just one, and it gave her awful nightmares.' "

Everyone looked at Muffy. She continued to study the cracks in the sidewalk.

The Brain read some more. " 'We started PAWS to save other kids,' added Millicent's husband, Ed. 'We're having a big rally for concerned parents at the library tomorrow. Afterward, all our supporters — young and old — can join us for a celebration at Wonder-World.' "

Buster was shocked. "Muffy, your mom and dad started PAWS?"

Muffy looked up. "Yes," she said.

"But why?" asked Francine.

Muffy bit her lip.

"Let me see that," Arthur said to the Brain.

The Brain gave him the newspaper.

Arthur read through the interview. "This isn't just any old WonderWorld party," he said. "Is it, Muffy? It's only for people who support PAWS."

Muffy shrugged. "Well, if you want to get technical . . ."

"Oh, no!" said Buster.

"We have to get our books back, Muffy," said Arthur. "Don't you understand?"

Muffy hesitated. Then she took a deep breath and folded her arms.

"You just have to decide which means more to you," she said. "WonderWorld — or a bunch of silly books. The choice is yours."

Chapter 7

● ● ● ● ● ● ● ● ● ● ● ●

"I don't know what's so complicated," said D.W. She put out her hands as though she were balancing things in a scale. "Some creepy books here. Free WonderWorld here." She lowered her WonderWorld hand to her knees, as though it was holding something heavy. The other hand shot up. "No contest."

She and Arthur were sitting in the living room. Arthur had told her about the problem with Muffy and her parents.

"It's not that simple," said Arthur.

D.W. laughed. "It is to me. You know how great WonderWorld is. They have the best roller coaster. People throw up and everything. What do you think, Kate?"

Their baby sister was watching from her playpen. Her hands were going up and down.

"See, Arthur?" said D.W. "Even Kate knows the right thing to do. And she's just a baby."

"The right thing to do about what?" asked Mrs. Read, taking a break from her work.

"Arthur gets to go to WonderWorld for free," said D.W.

"Really?" said Mrs. Read. "How did that come about?"

Arthur told her.

"I see," said his mother. "Well, Arthur, for someone going to WonderWorld, you don't look very happy."

Arthur sighed. "As I was trying to tell D.W., it's not that simple. I don't want to miss Muffy's party. But I don't want to lose my favorite books, either. And it's not really right to go if I don't support PAWS."

Mrs. Read nodded. "It's a difficult situation, Arthur. It's like a balance sheet. There are pluses and minuses. When you add everything up, you have to do what you think is right — even if it means making a sacrifice."

Arthur wandered outside to think some more. Why did sticking up for what you believe in have to be so difficult?

"I wish I knew what everyone else was thinking," Arthur muttered.

"I'll tell you what I'm thinking," said his father from the garage. "My life's an open book. A cookbook, that is." Mr. Read was busy with a huge catering job. But right now, he was looking through boxes.

"I wish there was a book where I could

look up the answers to hard questions," Arthur said.

He explained the situation to his father.

"That would be a good book to have," his father agreed. "Probably a best-seller." He opened a box. "Ah, here's what I was looking for."

He pulled out a clown costume. "Just what I need for this afternoon's children's hospital benefit."

He began putting the costume on.

"What if I'm the only one who decides to protest PAWS?" said Arthur. "What if all my friends decide to go to Wonder-World instead?"

Mr. Read adjusted his bald wig. "Can't be afraid to look foolish for something you believe in. Give me that rubber nose, please."

Arthur handed it to him. Then he sat down to think.

Bllaaattttt!

Arthur jumped up.

"Oh, thanks," said his father. "I wondered where that whoopee cushion was." Mr. Read put it in his pocket.

He looked at his watch.

"I've got to be going. Remember one thing, Arthur. I know you want to do what your friends are doing. But look at me."

Arthur stared at his father in his clown suit.

"Sometimes clowns work as a team." His father shook hands with a bunch of imaginary clowns around him. "And sometimes they stand under the spotlight all by themselves." He made a little bow.

Arthur sighed. And sometimes clowns looked sad, the way he felt right now.

Chapter 8

• • • • • • • • • • • •

At the library the next morning, the Crosswires stood at the top of the steps. Muffy kept ducking behind her parents, but they kept pulling her out in front of them.

A crowd of kids and parents was gathered around them.

Mr. Crosswire spoke into a portable microphone. "Thank you all for coming. I'm Ed Crosswire of Crosswire Motors, corner of Park and Lakewood, open most nights till ten. But I'm not doing this for me. I'm doing it to save our kids!"

His words were met by cheers and polite applause.

Off to the side, Arthur stood with his mother. He was holding up a sign that said, KEEP YOUR PAWS OFF OUR BOOKS!

Nobody seemed to be paying attention.

"I don't see anyone," said Arthur. "I guess WonderWorld wins."

"Don't be too sure," said Mrs. Read. "There's still time."

"This is our little girl," Ed Crosswire continued. He held up Muffy's hand. "We started PAWS because of her, but we care about all of you as well."

At that moment Buster, Francine, the Brain, and Sue Ellen came around the corner. They were holding signs over their heads.

OBEY THE LAWS — NOT PAWS!

CLOSE THE BOOK ON PAWS!

"You're here!" said Arthur. "I was beginning to wonder."

"Sorry we're late," said the Brain. "We stopped for more signatures."

He held out the petition sheets. There were now dozens and dozens of names.

"So who's going to give these to Mr. Crosswire?" Buster asked.

"You do it," said the Brain.

"Not me," said Buster. "You do it."

"Who?" said Sue Ellen.

"Not you," said Francine. "How about Arthur?"

"Yeah!"

"Good idea."

"Well, Arthur . . . ," said the Brain.

Arthur took a deep breath. "All right," he said. "I'll do it!"

Holding the petitions under one arm, he worked his way through the crowd.

No Ferris wheel. No sno-cones. No roller coaster.

"Excuse me. Excuse me. Coming through."

No cotton candy. No bumper cars. No haunted house.

At the top of the steps, Arthur stopped in front of Mr. Crosswire. He would be sorry to miss all those great things at WonderWorld. But this was more important.

"If we don't take a stand now, we will have failed in our trust. We must —"

"Excuse me, please, Mr. Crosswire," said Arthur. "We need to talk."

"Not now, Arthur. I'm on a roll."

"That's just it, Mr. Crosswire. You're rolling right over our rights. It's not fair. Speaking for the kids, we really want our books back. We've got these signatures of support —"

"That's nice, Arthur. I admire your spirit. But believe me, this is for your own good! These books are trouble with a capital *T*."

"Have you read them?" asked a voice from the crowd.

Arthur turned around. That voice was familiar.

Surprisingly, it was familiar to Ed Crosswire, too. He looked out over the crowd. He seemed a little confused.

Arthur wondered what would happen next.

Chapter 9

. . . .

"Who is that?" asked Ed Crosswire.

The rest of the crowd was silent.

"Answer the question," said the voice. "Have you read the books you're condemning?"

The crowd pulled back to reveal the speaker. Arthur recognized her. She was the woman he had spoken with in the park.

Mr. Crosswire cleared his throat. "I am proud to say that I wouldn't read these books if you paid me!"

The woman sighed. "I'm not surprised," she said.

Mr. Crosswire looked startled. "Why, I

know you. . . . You're Miss McWord, my grade-school English teacher."

"Yes, I am, Edward." She walked up the steps. "I'm glad to see your memory hasn't failed you — even if your common sense has."

"Miss McWord, I assure you I have every bit as much common sense as I ever did."

She stood beside him. "That may be true," she admitted. "I see you haven't changed. You never were much of a reader. Can you appreciate how hard a writer works to create stories kids will like to read? Each story is like a seed, Edward. If a child reads one, the seed may grow into the desire to read another. That's something every writer hopes for."

Mr. Crosswire crossed his arms. "Oh, really? Miss McWord, you were certainly a fine teacher. But what makes you such an expert about what writers hope for?"

"Well, I'm a writer myself."

"Oh. I'm sure we're all delighted to hear that." Mr. Crosswire hesitated. "Anything we'd know?"

Miss McWord straightened Mr. Crosswire's jacket and flicked some lint from his shoulder. "Nothing you've read, Edward, considering your common sense and all. But since you've asked, I'm the author of the Scare-Your-Pants-Off Club books."

"You!" said Mr. Crosswire, turning pale. He had a sudden vision of Miss McWord walking him down to the principal's office.

"You?" said Arthur.

"Her?" Francine, Buster, Sue Ellen, and the Brain said together.

The woman nodded. "E. A. D'Poe is my pen name."

Muffy nearly exploded with excitement. "Ms. D'Poe!" she cried. "I'm your number-one fan! I have all your books.

Could I have your —" Her parents glared at her. "Oooops!"

She clasped her hand across her mouth as her parents surrounded her.

"You read them all?" said her father.

"And just when did you do that?" asked her mother. "Mary Alice Crosswire, you've got some fancy explaining to do."

"Uh-oh!" said Muffy.

"If you've read all of these books," said Mrs. Crosswire, "then obviously it wasn't one of them that gave you the nightmare. What was it?"

"Um, well . . ." Muffy hated it when her mother sounded like a detective.

"Just a minute, here," said Mr. Crosswire. He stared at Muffy. "Now I know who ate my quart of Haasen-Pfeffer ice cream."

"And then was afraid to admit it," said her mother. "Mary Alice, you know eating like that gives you bad dreams."

"We're very disappointed in you," said her father.

"And I'm disappointed in you, too," Muffy's mother said to her husband. "What were you doing with a quart of that ice cream, anyway?"

"Well, I . . ."

Arthur almost smiled. Muffy and her father were both standing with their heads hanging low. They looked very much alike.

Miss McWord cleared her throat. "I hate to interrupt a promising family squabble, but we've still got some business to settle. Edward, maybe you can take your foot out of your mouth long enough to listen to one of my stories. That way you can make an informed decision about who should be reading them."

"Oh. Yes. Excellent idea."

At this particular moment, anything was better than facing his wife.

Chapter 10

* * * * * * * * * * * *

"And since that night, nobody has dared to steal anything from the haunted hamburger stand again."

Miss McWord put down her book.

The crowd clapped and cheered. Among the loudest fans was Ed Cross-wire.

"Well, Daddy?" Muffy asked.

He sighed. "I guess I shouldn't have tried to stop you kids from reading books without knowing *the whole story* myself."

"Maybe," said Miss McWord, "you have changed some, after all, Edward."

"So can we have our books back, Mr. Crosswire?" Arthur asked.

"I will disband PAWS on one condition," said Mr. Crosswire.

Everyone fell silent.

"And that condition is?" said Muffy.

"That Miss McWord will read us another story." Mr. Crosswire looked at her. "Please?"

"Yes!"

"Another one!"

"All right!"

Miss McWord smiled, something she didn't do very often. She cracked open another book.

"No one in the village knew why the old man lived all alone, deep in the dark woods. Only the animals of the forest knew his secret. . . ."

Arthur sat back and closed his eyes as a familiar chill crept up his spine.

Arthur
Makes the Team

Chapter 1

Buster and Arthur were walking along the sidewalk with their baseball gloves. As they walked, they tossed a ball back and forth.

"So, do you think you'll be good at baseball?" Buster asked.

Arthur shrugged. "I hope so," he said. He didn't want to admit to being nervous. He hadn't played last year, like some of the other kids.

"Did you learn a lot last year?" he asked.

Buster laughed. "Did I? Let me show you. Run out for a long catch."

Arthur trotted past a tree.

Buster waved him on. "Farther . . . farther . . . Okay, stand there. Are you ready? See if you can catch the famous Buster Ball."

"Ready!" said Arthur. He held up his glove.

Buster threw the ball as hard as he could. But instead of going toward Arthur, the ball shot up into a tree. It bounced around in the branches.

"I've got it," said Arthur, circling underneath.

The ball bounced down off one branch, then another, before rolling onto a roof.

"I've still got it," said Arthur, following the ball's every move.

The ball rolled down the roof and into the gutter. It shot out the bottom of the downspout, passed between Arthur's legs, and rolled into a storm drain.

"Oops!" said Arthur. "I guess I don't have it after all."

Buster looked down the drain. He sighed. "I lose more balls that way."

"That was a pretty amazing throw," said Arthur. "And you learned that in just one season?"

"I sure did. Don't worry — you'll catch on quickly. Just think: you're standing out there in the middle of the field. There's no one around."

"No one around," said Arthur.

"No place to hide," said Buster.

"No place to hide," Arthur repeated.

"At the crack of the bat, the ball is headed your way. Everyone is staring, watching your every move."

"My every move?" said Arthur.

"Of course," said Buster. "And not just your teammates. The other team is watching, too. And the crowd in the stands. Especially your family."

"My family?"

Buster nodded. "Sure. Parents. Grandparents. Sisters. Everybody comes to the games."

Arthur sighed. "Let me get this straight. I'm all alone in the middle of the field, and the whole world is watching whenever the ball comes to me."

"Pretty exciting, huh?" said Buster.

"I guess," said Arthur. *Exciting* wasn't actually the word he had in mind.

"And don't forget batting," said Buster.

"No, I wouldn't want to do that."

Buster crouched down in a batting stance. "It's just you and the pitcher. Nothing else matters. You raise your bat. Ready. Waiting. The pitch blazes in. You can feel the heat as the ball passes by."

Arthur swallowed. "You feel the heat?"

"Well, maybe not," Buster admitted. "But it's a tense moment."

"Because everyone is watching."

"Exactly."

"The umpire calls, 'Strike!' But that's

okay. It wasn't your pitch. But now you stand in."

"Stand in," said Arthur.

"It's another fastball. But this time you swing. The ball streaks like a rocket. It's a home run! You circle the bases to the cheers of the crowd."

"Just like that?" said Arthur.

"Well, not every time. But it could happen if you're lucky."

Arthur sighed. He didn't know if that would happen to him. But it was nice to think about.

Chapter 2

• • • • • • • • • • • •

At the ball field, a bunch of kids were huddled around the bulletin board, looking at the team rosters.

"I found my name," said Buster. "Let's see . . . Francine . . . Brain . . . Binky . . . Arthur. Yes! Yes! We're all on the Eagles together. Hey, this is going to be a great team. I can't wait to start pitching."

"Hey, I want to pitch!" said Francine.

"So do I," said the Brain.

"How will we choose?" asked Buster.

"Don't worry," said Francine. "The coach will decide."

"But Francine," said the Brain, "your father is the coach."

She smiled. "Funny how these things work out."

"How what things work out?" asked her father, coming up to join them. He had on his official Eagles hat and T-shirt.

"Nothing, Daddy," said Francine, smiling at him.

"I think I'm going to be sick," whispered Buster.

"I think you'll have company," the Brain whispered back.

The whole team — including Sue Ellen, Speedy, Fern, and Alex — sat down in the grass.

"I'm glad everyone could be here for our first practice," said the coach. "As most of you know, I'm Oliver Frensky, Francine's dad."

Francine gave Buster a big smile.

"Now, our motto is going to be

'Teamwork!'" the coach went on. "If you have a favorite position, you can start with that. But you'll all be moving around. Who's going to be our first pitcher?"

Buster, Francine, and the Brain all raised their hands.

"Excellent. We have a whole staff. Buster, why don't you go first?"

"But . . . but —," Francine sputtered.

"You'll get your turn," her father reassured her.

Everyone else took a position. Arthur ended up in right field. Nobody else seemed to want to be there.

"Heads up, everyone!" said the coach, waiting with a bat at home plate. "Go ahead, Buster."

Buster prepared to pitch. He twirled his arm around, shot out his leg, and threw as hard as he could.

Coach Frensky blinked.

"Where did the ball go?"

Buster wasn't sure. He was never sure with a Buster Ball. A moment later the ball came down and hit him on the head.

"Are you all right, Buster?" asked the coach.

Buster nodded.

"Good. Try again. But this time ease up a little. Don't wear your arm out the first day."

Buster nodded. He pitched again — and the ball sailed right over the plate. The coach lined a drive to Sue Ellen at third base.

After a few more pitches, it was Francine's turn. Her first pitches were high and outside. Her father fouled them off.

"Nice energy," he said. "Remember now, right over the plate."

Francine's next pitches were better. Her father batted them around the field.

Time for my fastball, thought Francine.

She gripped the ball firmly — and threw.

The ball sailed high over everything — her father, Binky, even the backstop.

"Well," said her father, "that was certainly over the plate."

"Way over," said Binky.

The coach cleared his throat. "All right, Francine, let's give someone else a chance."

The Brain took to the mound.

"Ready?" asked the coach.

"In a moment," said the Brain. He licked his finger and held it up to test the wind direction. Then he began scraping the mound with his sneaker.

"Is everything all right?" asked the coach.

"Oh, yes," said the Brain. "Proper footing is very important."

When he was finally ready, the Brain made his first careful pitch.

Coach Frensky hit a grounder to short-stop.

The Brain was pleased. He checked the wind and his footing again. He did that before every pitch, so he didn't get many in.

The last ball went to right field. It was a deep pop fly.

"I've got it!" said Arthur, moving backward. He leaped at what he thought was the right moment.

And missed.

The ball came down behind him.

"Almost!" said the coach. "Arthur, that was a very graceful leap."

Graceful? Arthur didn't feel graceful. He could feel his face getting red. He knew everyone was looking at him.

It was starting to look like the season would be a long one.

Chapter 3

• • • • • • • • • • •

Arthur stood in front of his bedroom mirror, tossing a ball up and down in his mitt.

His father stopped in the hall to watch him. "Ready for your next practice, Arthur?" he asked.

Arthur dropped the ball. "Oh, uh . . . yeah," he said.

Mr. Read stepped into the room. "Is everything okay?"

"Um, I guess. Practices have been hard."

"Really? Tell me about them."

"I'm not very comfortable yet. The other day I was playing second base. I fielded a sharp grounder, but I couldn't get it out of my glove. It was like the ball was stuck with glue."

"What did you do?" his father asked.

"Well, there was a force on at second, so I took off the glove and threw it to the shortstop, who was covering the bag."

"Was the throw in time?"

Arthur sighed. "The glove was. But the ball came out along the way and dribbled into the outfield. The runner ended up at third base."

"What did the coach say?" asked Mr. Read.

"He said I was ingenious. Very creative. He uses words like that a lot when I make a play."

Mr. Read sat down on the bed. "The coach has a good eye, Arthur. You just need to give it a little time."

Arthur wasn't so sure. "Everyone else just seems so far ahead of me. And I feel funny asking for help about stuff that everybody else knows already."

"Yes, well, most of them played last year, and you didn't. Having a head start makes a difference. I had kind of the same thing happen to me."

"You did?"

His father nodded. "It was when I first got interested in cooking. Of course, I didn't know I would end up as a caterer. I just liked experimenting with food. I was sick the first week and missed the class where the teacher explained how all the equipment worked. The next week I was too shy to ask questions. I just pretended I knew as much as everyone else."

"Did it work?" asked Arthur.

His father smiled. "For a few minutes. But then we had to make salad dressing in a blender. Everyone else knew that the lid needed to be locked a certain way. I didn't. So when I turned it on . . ."

Arthur gasped.

"You guessed it. The salad dressing ended up on everything and everyone else. It was quite a mess."

"Did you get in trouble?"

His father made a face. "For a moment I thought my life was over. The teacher was covered in goop. He shook his fist at me, and goop dropped off his hand onto the floor."

Arthur's mouth dropped open.

"The room was perfectly still. And then he started to laugh. 'This,' he said, 'is a good example of what I was talking about — *last week*.' "

Arthur sighed. "So you survived."

"Exactly. But I never tried to pretend I knew what I was doing again. And you shouldn't, either. Don't be afraid to ask for help or advice. You'll catch up soon enough."

Chapter 4

• • • • • • • • • • •

Coach Frensky was standing behind the backstop, watching his team warm up.

"Excuse me. Coach?"

The coach turned.

"I'm Buster's mother, Bitsy."

"Nice to meet you. Buster's a fine boy, a real sparkplug!"

"That's very nice to hear. I was just wondering . . . Is the ball very hard?"

"Well, no harder than any baseball."

"I see. I've just been wondering . . . What if it hits Buster?"

"Well, there's always some risk, but Buster's very quick. I'm sure —"

"And the baseball hats, are they made of wool? I think Buster's allergic to wool. If he's scratching, I don't think he'll be playing his best."

"We'll watch for scratching." Coach Frensky glanced at the bleachers. "Now, I'd recommend you find a seat, um, Bitsy. You don't want all the good ones to be taken."

"Do the seats often fill up for practice?"

Coach Frensky hesitated. "You never know," he said.

On the field, Arthur and Buster were throwing to each other. As Francine approached, Buster held up an imaginary microphone in front of her mouth.

"Excuse me, Slugger. Buster here for Action News. Think you'll top your record of forty-nine sky balls today?"

"Very funny," said Francine. "At least my throws go over the plate."

"Take it easy," said Arthur. "You're both on the same team, remember?"

"Stay out of this, Arthur," said Francine. "You need to concentrate all your attention on holding on to the ball."

"Oh, yeah?" Arthur put his hands on his hips — and the ball dropped out of his glove.

Francine laughed and moved onto the field.

"You know what you need, Arthur?" said Buster. "My never-fail, always-succeeds, one-hundred-percent guaranteed, secret good-luck charm."

He reached into his pocket and produced a shriveled carrot.

Arthur made a face.

"Use this and you can't miss," said Buster. He handed the carrot to Arthur.

"You're sure about this?" asked Arthur.

"One hundred percent absolutely double-sure guaranteed."

"Okay," said Arthur, and he put it in his pocket.

All during practice, Arthur fingered the good-luck charm. But since no tough balls were hit to him, he couldn't be sure if it was working. When Francine came up to bat, he crouched down to be ready.

Francine crushed the next pitch to deep right field. Arthur ran back, watching it the whole way.

"Watch the fence!" Buster yelled.

Arthur stopped short and looked up. The ball was coming down. He reached out to catch it.

The ball bounced off his glove and went over the fence.

"Home run!" shouted Francine, rounding the bases.

Arthur frowned.

Later, Arthur returned the carrot to Buster.

"Here," he said. "I think it's broken. Or maybe it's run out of luck."

Then he walked away.

Buster examined the carrot and shrugged. He took a bite and put the rest in his pocket.

Chapter 5

• • • • • • • • • • • •

After practice, Coach Frensky led the team to the Sugar Bowl.

"You've been working hard," he said. "Time for a little reward."

Arthur was the last in, just behind Buster. It was amazing to him that everyone else could be so happy and relaxed. Most of the kids had made the same kind of mistakes on the field that he had. Somehow it didn't seem to bother them so much.

"A great practice deserves ice cream!" said the coach. He went off to see about getting some tables pushed together.

"Are you prepared, Arthur?" Francine asked.

Arthur eyed her cautiously. "What do you mean?"

"An ice cream cone can be tricky. If you're not careful, you might drop it."

A lot of the kids laughed.

"Don't listen to her, Arthur," said Buster. "You're entitled to ice cream just as much as the rest of us. If you want, though, I'll hold it for you."

"Thanks, Buster," said Arthur. "I think."

Once their orders were taken, everyone sat down. Arthur, Francine, Buster, the Brain, and Binky were all at the same table.

Francine was busy complaining. "Our problem is batting," she said. "We don't have good batting."

Arthur had struck out twice that afternoon. He was swinging too soon, the coach had told him.

"I think we look pretty good," said Buster.

Francine laughed. "With your eyesight, I'm not surprised."

"There's nothing wrong with my eyesight," said Buster. "I eat plenty of carrots."

Arthur fiddled with his glasses. Sometimes it was hard to keep his eye on the ball.

"Some people," said Binky, "have to learn how to stop the ball." He pounded his chest. "Even if you can't keep it in your glove, you keep it in front of you."

Arthur looked down at his legs. Balls had passed through them so often, they felt like goalposts.

"If we concentrate on learning the fundamentals," said the Brain, "our chances of winning will improve over time."

"I suppose," said Francine. "But they don't look too good right now."

"Well," said the Brain, "it would help if you stopped throwing the ball over Fern's head."

"I didn't do that!" said Francine. "And she was standing too close, anyway."

Coach Frensky arrived at the table with two pitchers of soda.

"Hey!" he said, frowning. "I don't want to hear any talk like that. We're a team, remember?"

Everyone shut up.

Coach Frensky surveyed the table. "Where's Arthur?" he asked.

"He was here a second ago," said Buster.

"Probably went for napkins," said Binky.

"Look!" said the Brain. He pointed out the window.

Arthur was slinking up the street. A line of drips from his ice cream cone trailed behind him.

"I guess he wasn't in the mood for talk," said Francine.

"I guess not," said her father. But he stood there thinking it over for a long time.

Chapter 6

• • • • • • • • • • •

At dinner, Arthur sat quietly at the table. He barely touched his hamburger. He wasn't very hungry.

The same could not be said for D.W. Her hamburger was half gone, and she was munching away on corn-on-the-cob.

"I see you favor the rolling approach," said her father.

D.W. looked confused. "What's that?"

"It's when you roll your corn around before moving it down a little and rolling it some more."

D.W. stopped to look at her corn. "It's the best way," she said.

"Don't be so sure," said her mother. "Some people favor the typewriter approach — eating all the way across in a row, turning the cob a little, and then starting a new row."

D.W. shrugged. "My way is better," she said.

"For you, sweetie," said her mother.

"What do you think, Arthur?" asked Mr. Read.

"Huh?"

Arthur hadn't been listening.

"Which way do you like to eat corn?" his father asked.

Arthur sighed. "Whichever way you make the fewest mistakes."

Mr. Read looked confused. "I'm not sure you can make a mistake eating corn," he said. "True, you could miss a kernel here or there, but I'm not sure that really counts."

"Arthur's not talking about corn," said D.W. "He's talking about baseball."

"How are your practices going?" asked his mother.

"Not too well," said Arthur. "I know what to do in my head. But my body doesn't always go along."

"That's perfectly natural," said Mr. Read. "Be patient, Arthur. You're paying attention, and that's what's important. Baseball is ninety-nine percent concentration."

"Sometimes it feels like everyone is concentrating on what a bad job I'm doing. Not Coach Frensky, though. He's always encouraging. He says I'm making good progress."

"Which parts do you feel comfortable with?" asked his mother.

Arthur stopped to think. "I can throw okay. And when the ball is hit to me, I can get to the right place . . ."

"But you can't catch the ball," said D.W.

"D.W.!" said her father. "You'll catch

more than a ball if you say another word."

D.W. went back to her corn.

Arthur stared at his plate. "She's right," he said. "It's what everyone else says."

"Nonsense," said Mr. Read. "I'm sure you're making a positive contribution. There are probably people talking about it even now."

"You really think so?"

Mr. Read nodded. "Absolutely. So you'd better eat up. Ballplayers need their strength."

Arthur nodded. With their first game coming up, he wanted to be ready. He picked up his corn in both hands. With a look at D.W., he began eating it across in rows.

Chapter 7

• • • • • • • • • • • •

"It's painful," Francine was saying.

She was sitting in her living room with Muffy.

"What's painful?" Muffy asked. "No, don't tell me. It has something to do with baseball."

Francine was surprised. "How did you know?" she asked.

"Because that's all you talk about lately. Double plays . . . making the cutoff . . . guarding the plate."

"Well, it's important," said Francine.

Muffy yawned. "Not to me. I could

understand it better if you thought your team was any good."

Francine punched her pillow. "Don't remind me. Buster can't throw. The Brain takes too long for everything. And as for Arthur . . ." She shook her head.

"Couldn't you promote him or something?" said Muffy. "Make him president or general manager? Anything to get him off the field. My daddy's always talking about people getting kicked upstairs in business."

Francine hadn't thought of that. "It might work. We could give Arthur lots of interesting jobs. He'd be really busy."

"Give him a fancy title and some fringe benefits," said Muffy. "You know, like free parking and paid vacations. My daddy says those are important."

Francine was nodding. "Yes, yes," she said. "Arthur would probably like all that."

"Arthur would probably like *what?*" asked her father, coming in from the kitchen.

"We were just discussing the team, Daddy."

The coach smiled. "We're pulling together nicely," he said. "Still a few kinks, of course, but that's only normal."

Francine smiled at him. "Speaking of kinks, Daddy, Muffy suggested a way to get Arthur off the field: promote him to assistant coach."

"Oh, really?" said Mr. Frensky.

Francine folded her fingers together. "What do you say, Daddy? Please! I can't even throw straight because I'm worrying what dumb thing Arthur's going to do next."

"That sounds serious," said her father. "You're worried about Arthur, aren't you?"

"Why, yes . . . Can't you see that?"

Her father stroked his chin. "It's natural

for you to be concerned. After all, he is one of your best friends."

"Then you'll do it?"

Her father thought for a moment. "As coach, I have to look beyond any one player's needs. I have to consider the whole team."

"Of course," said Francine. "I think the whole team would benefit."

"You have to stand way back to get the big picture," said her father. "I may not have been seeing everything myself. Thank you, Francine."

"So you'll promote him?"

Her father shook his head. "No, no, I've got a better idea."

"Oh?" Francine didn't want a better idea. She liked her idea just the way it was.

Her father rubbed his chin. "Yes . . . definitely a better idea. I'm not going to promote Arthur. I'm going to promote you instead."

"What? You mean you want to get me off the field?"

"Not exactly," said her father, grinning broadly. "I had a different promotion in mind."

Francine looked at him suspiciously. Whenever her father used that tone, something odd was bound to happen.

Chapter 8

• • • • • • • • • • • •

Arthur stood in his garage, throwing a tennis ball against the wall.

Bounce-bounce-catch.

Bounce-bounce-catch.

Too bad they don't use these in the games, he thought.

"Hi, Arthur."

Francine stood in the driveway.

Arthur ignored her.

Bounce-bounce-catch.

Bounce-bounce-catch.

"Come on, Arthur. You can't ignore me forever."

Arthur stopped bouncing the ball.

"What brings you here, Francine? No, don't tell me. I'll bet you've thought up some new insults since yesterday."

Francine's face reddened. "Actually, I came over with some news. My father has made me the new assistant coach."

"Congratulations. Would that be Assistant Coach in Charge of Criticism?"

"No, no . . . Look, Arthur, maybe I have gotten a little carried away lately. I'm sorry. But now my dad says I have to make sure the team works together."

She took out a baseball.

"And my first project is you."

"Me?" Arthur crossed his arms. "What if I don't want to be a project?"

"Would you rather be teased and feel embarrassed all the time?"

Arthur sighed. He picked up his glove, and they went into the backyard.

"Ready?" said Francine.

She threw the ball high overhead.

Arthur circled underneath it. "I've got it! I've got it!"

The ball landed five feet away.

Francine smothered a giggle. "Let's try again," she said.

She picked up the ball and threw it up into the air.

Arthur raised his glove.

"That's it," said Francine. "Get under it!"

Arthur followed the ball's path — until the sun blinded him. He raised his arm to block the sun — and the ball hit him on the head.

"Ouch!"

"Well," said Francine, "at least you were under it. Look." She came over to show him. "Use your glove to keep the sun out of your eyes. That also puts the glove in a better place to catch the ball. Don't think about doing everything at once. Break it into steps."

"Oh," said Arthur. "I see."

"One more time . . ."

She threw the ball up again. This time Arthur used his glove to block the sun. He circled and circled — and caught the ball.

Arthur smiled.

Francine smiled, too.

They practiced a few more times.

"I think you're getting the hang of this, Arthur."

He thought so, too.

"Thanks, Francine. You know, you might take a little advice yourself."

"Me? About what?"

"About pitching your fastball." He crouched down into a catching stance. "Come on, fire it in here."

Francine threw the ball. It sailed over Arthur's head, Pal's doghouse, and the fence.

While Francine went to get the ball, Arthur stopped to think.

"All right," said Francine, returning to her position. "Let's try again."

"Wait a minute," said Arthur. "You know, Francine, maybe you should think about your pitching the same way you told me to think about my catching?"

"What do you mean?"

"Breaking it into steps. Look, when you throw, you need to push off with your legs first and use your shoulder. And even after you release the ball, you still have to follow through."

"How do you know so much about it?"

Arthur looked a little embarrassed.

"Well?"

"Actually, it was D.W. I heard her explaining the whole thing to my mother."

"You're telling me to take advice from D.W.?"

Arthur shrugged. "Nobody has to know — especially D.W. What have you got to lose?"

"All right," said Francine. She got ready.

"Legs . . . shoulder . . ."

She fired the ball in at Arthur.

"Ouch!" he shouted. He pulled his hand out of his glove and shook it. "That was a real fastball."

Francine looked pleased. "It was, wasn't it?" she said. "Thanks for the tip."

"You're welcome," said Arthur.

Francine paused. "I really am sorry I teased you so much before."

Arthur nodded. "Well, you do overdo it sometimes."

"If I ever overdo it again, let me know. Deal?"

"Deal."

"It was kind of your fault, though."

"My fault?" said Arthur. "How do you figure that?"

"Well, if you hadn't kept dropping balls, I wouldn't have teased you."

"Oh, yeah? Well at least when I throw a ball, it lands in the same neighborhood."

As Francine started to answer, she suddenly froze — and laughed.

Arthur laughed, too. "Here we go again . . . ," he said.

Chapter 9

• • • • • • • • • • •

Coach Frensky paced back and forth in front of his bench. "Okay, team, this is our first game. The Penguins are pretty good, I hear." He took a deep breath. "But I want you to play just the way you have in practice. Just go out and have fun."

The coach clapped his hands. "Okay, team. Let's go!"

The Eagles took the field. In the first inning, a ball was hit sharply on the ground to Arthur. He fielded it cleanly and threw to second base.

"All right, Arthur!" said Buster.

His parents cheered from the bleachers.

"That's my brother," D.W. told everyone around her. "I taught him everything he knows."

The next four innings passed quickly. Each team scored two runs. In the bottom of the fifth, Arthur came up to bat for the second time. He had walked before.

Now he rapped a single to center.

"Way to go, Arthur!" yelled Francine from the bench.

Buster was next. He fouled off two pitches but swung all the way around on the third.

"Strike three!" shouted the umpire.

Mrs. Baxter stood up in the stands and clapped. "Way to swing, Buster!" she called out.

The Brain pitched the last two innings. The sixth was scoreless, but in the top of the seventh, the Penguins scored a run to take the lead. Then, with one out, their fifth batter singled to first and reached third on an overthrow.

The next batter came up.

The Brain licked his finger, testing the wind direction.

Then he threw to the plate.

Thwack!

It was a deep fly ball.

"It's yours, Arthur," Francine called from second base.

"I can't watch," said Buster in left field.

Arthur backpedaled over the grass. He blinked a few times, but he never took his eye off the ball. Remember what Francine said, he told himself. He shielded his eyes with his glove.

Arthur reached the fence. The ball was coming down fast.

Plopp.

Arthur had caught it.

"Relay!" shouted Francine.

Arthur threw the ball. Francine caught it and spun around. The runner had tagged up at third and was heading for home plate.

Binky was waiting.

"Throw it!" he called out.

Francine wasn't pitching, but she knew she had to throw a perfect fastball. She planted her feet firmly and fired to him.

The runner was sliding in. Binky swept him with the tag.

"Out!" called the umpire.

Arthur's team trotted in from the field. They were down one run, but they still had their last turn at bat.

The game wasn't over yet.

Chapter 10

• • • • • • • • • • • • •

Everyone on the bench was watching the field.

Sue Ellen was up first. The first pitch was a ball.

"Wait for yours!" shouted Francine.

Sue Ellen nodded. She stepped back into the batter's box.

In came the pitch.

Sue Ellen swung hard — and lined the ball into left field.

Coach Frensky whistled. "All right! The tieing run's on first."

Fern was the next batter. She hit a

blooper to right field, advancing Sue Ellen to second.

"Keep it going," said the coach.

Now Binky came to the plate. He tapped the dirt from his cleats and cocked his bat.

In came the pitch.

Binky swung hard, but a little early. The ball went deep to right field, but it was caught just before the fence. He was out, but Sue Ellen tagged up at second and ran to third.

Buster was up next.

"Just make good contact," said the coach. "A single ties it. Keep us alive."

Buster nodded.

He watched the first two pitches pass. One ball and one strike.

The third pitch came in. Buster jumped on it.

The ball popped up a mile high. Everyone looked up.

The pitcher called for the catch.

Arthur held his breath. Maybe the pitcher would trip on the grass or be blinded by the sun or get a sudden itch in his back and scratch it with his glove.

Thummp!

The ball was caught. The game was over. The Penguins had won.

Buster trudged back to the dugout as the other team ran off the field, cheering in victory.

"Good effort, Buster," said the coach. "I thought that one was heading for the fence."

"Me, too," said Arthur. "Good try."

Francine stormed over to Buster. "Boy, Buster, all we needed was one little hit, and you couldn't —"

Arthur coughed.

Francine looked at him. "— and you couldn't . . . have made a better try. Good job."

She patted Buster on the shoulder.

Their families gathered round for a few minutes before everyone headed home.

Arthur, Francine, and Buster were the last to leave. They replayed the whole game in their minds.

"We really did pretty well," said Arthur. "And the season's just starting."

"That's right," said Francine. "The next game will be better."

Buster shrugged. "I hope so," he said.

"You know, Buster," said Arthur, "Francine gave me some baseball tips the other day. Maybe she could do the same for you."

"I don't know . . . ," said Buster.

"Just think about all the power you put into your Buster Ball," said Francine.

Buster brightened.

"We just need to find a way to get that

power into your bat. We'll have to get to-gether and —"

"What about now?" Buster asked.

"Now?" Francine looked around. The field was empty.

Buster grabbed a bat and went to home plate. "Come on, come on, what are you waiting for?"

"Arthur?" whispered Francine.

"Yes?"

"Thanks for stopping me before I teased Buster the way I teased you."

"You're welcome. And thanks for help-ing me with my game. See? Teamwork is the answer."

Francine nodded. "Yeah. But you know, soccer season is coming up. And if you stink at that, I get to tease you all over again."

With that, she went to the pitcher's mound, leaving Arthur to go behind the plate.

"All right, Buster, pay attention. First thing we do . . ."

Arthur smiled. He wouldn't say that Francine would *never* learn.

But it definitely was going to take some time.

Marc Brown is the creator of the best-selling Arthur Adventure book series and codeveloper of the number one children's PBS television series, *Arthur*. He has also created a second book series, featuring D.W., Arthur's little sister, as well as numerous other books for children. Marc Brown lives with his family in Hingham, Massachusetts, and on Martha's Vineyard.

• • • • • • • • • •